More **Dark Man** books:

First series

The Dark Fire of Doom	978-184167-417-9
Destiny in the Dark	978-184167-422-3
The Dark Never Hides	978-184167-419-3
The Face in the Dark Mirror	978-184167-411-7
Fear in the Dark	978-184167-412-4
Escape from the Dark	978-184167-416-2
Danger in the Dark	978-184167-415-5
The Dark Dreams of Hell	978-184167-418-6
The Dark Side of Magic	978-184167-414-8
The Dark Glass	978-184167-421-6
The Dark Waters of Time	978-184167-413-1
The Shadow in the Dark	978-184167-420 9

Second series

The Dark Candle	978-184167-603-6
The Dark Machine	978-184167-601-2
The Dark Words	978-184167-602-9
Dying for the Dark	978-184167-604-3
Killer in the Dark	978-184167-605-0
The Day is Dark	978-184167-606-7
The Dark River	978-184167-745-3
The Bridge of Dark Tears	67-746-0
The Past is Dark	67-747-7
Playing the	67-748-4
The Dark M	67-749-1
The Dark G	67-750-7

Dark Man

The Shadow in the Dark
by Peter Lancett
illustrated by Jan Pedroietta

Published by Ransom Publishing Ltd.
51 Southgate Street, Winchester, Hampshire SO23 9EH
www.ransom.co.uk

ISBN   978 184167 420 9
First published in 2006
Second printing 2008

Copyright © 2006 Ransom Publishing Ltd.

Text copyright © 2006 Peter Lancett
Illustrations copyright © 2006 Jan Pedroietta

Printed in China through Colorcraft Ltd., Hong Kong.

Set 2: Book 4

Dark Man

The
Shadow
in the
Dark

by Peter Lancett

illustrated by Jan Pedroietta

Ransom

Chapter One:
Where the Iron Melts

It is loud here, where the Dark Man
stands.

This place is like a man-made hell.

Bang! Bang! Then clank! Clank!

Sounds of metal hitting metal.

Steam hisses from black pipes.

Yellow sparks burst into the night, casting shadows.

It is a place where steel is made, and iron melts.

This is why the Dark Man is here.

A girl told him that a Golden Cup is hidden "where the iron melts."

This Golden Cup has great power.

The evil Shadow Masters also seek it.

Chapter Two:
The Demon

The Dark Man hears a hiss behind him.

He turns.

This is not steam from a pipe.

This is a demon!

He has been followed!

The demon is like a shadow and is hard
to see.

Talons strike the Dark Man's face.

The Dark Man tries to fight but the
demon is fast.

He cannot see it in the darkness.

The talons strike again.

He turns and runs.

He needs to find a better place to fight.

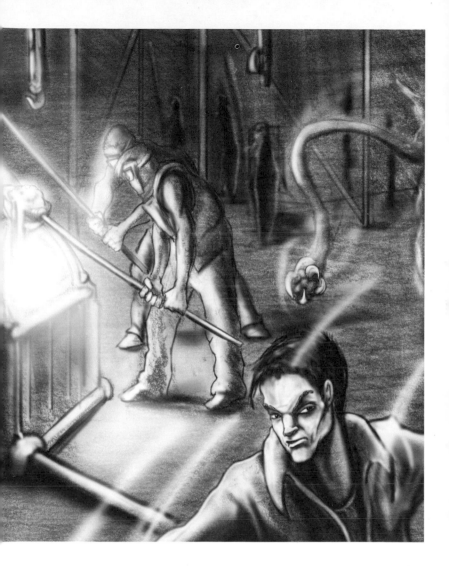

He runs past men, working with glowing metal.

They do not notice him.

He hears the hiss of the demon close behind him.

Chapter Three:
In the Darkness

He still cannot see a good place to stand and fight.

Then he sees something that makes him stop.

On a walkway high above, he sees a Shadow Master!

The Shadow Master is not alone.

Someone else is there, hidden in the dark.

As he looks up, the Dark Man is thrown to the ground.

The demon stands above him, ready to strike.

The Dark Man rolls away.

Then he sees something.

A golden object, hidden behind pipes.

He grabs the object.

It is the Golden Cup!

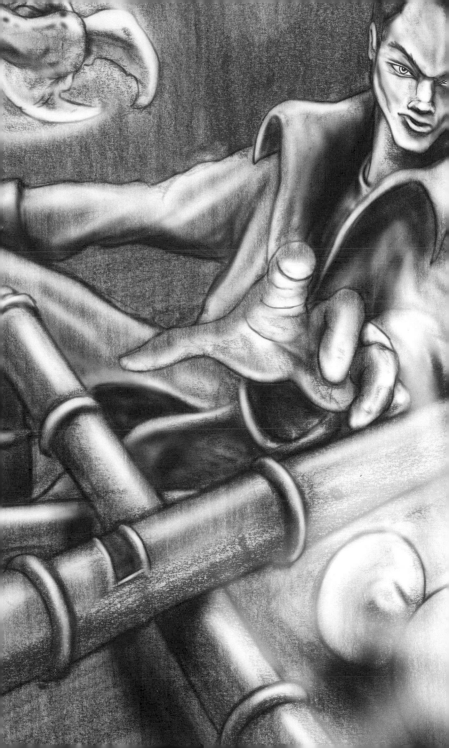

Chapter Four:
Lost

The demon screams and dives for the Cup.

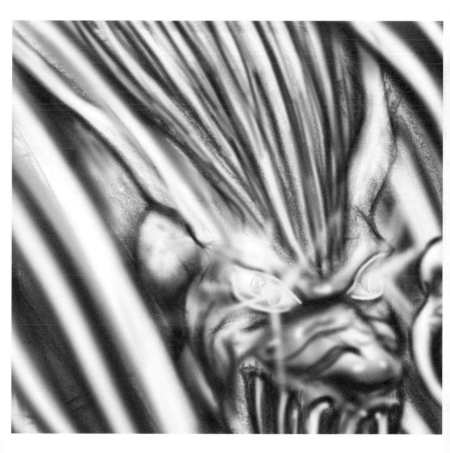

The Dark Man is fast and escapes.

He runs to the side of a huge well of molten steel.

By its light, he can see the demon.

The demon leaps and he jumps back.

There are screams as the demon falls into the molten metal.

But it has grabbed the Golden Cup!

The Cup is lost, but at least the Shadow
Masters do not have it.

The Dark Man looks up to the walkway.

The Shadow Master has gone.

Sadness flows within the Dark Man.

He knows who was with the Shadow Master.

It was a girl he once loved.

The Shadow Masters took her from him,
long ago.

Now he knows he will be alone forever.

The author

photograph: Rachel Ottewill

Peter Lancett used to work in the movies. Then he worked in the city. Now he writes horror stories for a living. "It beats having a proper job," he says.